Tick Tock

Tick Tock

David K. Williams
Illustrated by Laura Ovresat

Green Light Readers
Harcourt, Inc.
Orlando Austin New York San Diego Toronto London

Tick, tock!
ticked the clock.

Call Kim and Mick.
We need help quick!

Pass me the mop.
We can't stop.

Tick, tock!
ticked the clock.

Kim picks up pots—
lots and lots!

Mick is picking up hats.
Todd is packing up mats.

Tick, tock!
ticked the clock.

Pick up that sock.
Look at the clock!

Mom's home now.
We did it. Wow!

Hickory, Dickory, Dock

Make a paper plate clock.

paper plate

construction paper

crayons or markers

brass fasteners

scissors

1. Number the plate like a clock. You can draw other decorations on it, too!

2. Draw two arrows on construction paper to be the hands of the clock. Cut them out with scissors.

3. Put the hands in the middle with a brass fastener.

4. Say the rhyme "Hickory, Dickory, Dock."

Hickory, dickory, dock,

The mouse ran up the clock.

The clock struck one,

The mouse ran down,

Hickory, dickory, dock.

Walk
With Me

The kids in this story worked together to help clean up the house. Work together with a partner in this game.

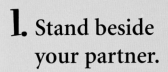

1. Stand beside
your partner.

2. Use a scarf to tie
one of your legs
to one of your
partner's legs.

3. Try walking or
hopping.

Share with classmates what happens.
What did you learn about working together?

Meet the Illustrator

Laura Ovresat has two little girls who love to make messes. In fact, it's their specialty! When Laura painted the pictures for this book, she had a dream that her kids and their friends cleaned up the entire house. The pictures she painted came from her dream.

Laura Ovresat

For information about permission to reproduce selections from this book, please write to Permissions, Houghton Mifflin Harcourt Publishing Company 215 Park Avenue South NY, NY 10003.

www.hmhbooks.com

First Green Light Readers edition 2006

Green Light Readers is a trademark of Harcourt, Inc., registered in the United States of America and/or other jurisdictions.

Library of Congress Cataloging-in-Publication Data
Williams, David K.
Tick tock/by David K. Williams; illustrated by Laura Ovresat.
p. cm.
"Green Light Readers."
Summary: Four friends race the clock to clean the house before Mom gets home.
[1. Housekeeping—Fiction. 2. Time—Fiction. 3. Stories in rhyme.]
I. Ovresat, Laura, ill. II. Title. III. Series.
PZ8.3.W6735Tic 2006
[E]—dc22 2005006938
ISBN-13: 978-0152-05581-3 ISBN-10: 0-15-205581-9
ISBN-13: 978-0152-05605-6 (pb) ISBN-10: 0-15-205605-X (pb)

SCP 10 9 8 7 6 5
4500409618

Ages 4–6
Grades: K–1
Guided Reading Level: C–D
Reading Recovery Level: 3–4

Green Light Readers
For the reader who's ready to GO!

"A must-have for any family with a beginning reader."—*Boston Sunday Herald*

"You can't go wrong with adding several copies of these terrific books to your beginning-to-read collection."—*School Library Journal*

"A winner for the beginner."—*Booklist*

Five Tips to Help Your Child Become a Great Reader

1. Get involved. Reading aloud to and with your child is just as important as encouraging your child to read independently.

2. Be curious. Ask questions about what your child is reading.

3. Make reading fun. Allow your child to pick books on subjects that interest her or him.

4. Words are everywhere—not just in books. Practice reading signs, packages, and cereal boxes with your child.

5. Set a good example. Make sure your child sees YOU reading.

Why Green Light Readers Is the Best Series for Your New Reader

• Created exclusively for beginning readers by some of the biggest and brightest names in children's books

• Reinforces the reading skills your child is learning in school

• Encourages children to read—and finish—books by themselves

• Offers extra enrichment through fun, age-appropriate activities unique to each story

• Incorporates characteristics of the Reading Recovery program used by educators

• Developed with Harcourt School Publishers and credentialed educational consultants